B.T. Tanner

The Negro's Origin

B.T. Tanner

The Negro's Origin

Reprint of the original, first published in 1869.

1st Edition 2022 | ISBN: 978-3-37504-422-0

Verlag (Publisher): Salzwasser Verlag GmbH, Zeilweg 44, 60439 Frankfurt, Deutschland
Vertretungsberechtigt (Authorized to represent): E. Roepke, Zeilweg 44, 60439 Frankfurt, Deutschland
Druck (Print): Books on Demand GmbH, In de Tarpen 42, 22848 Norderstedt, Deutschland

THE

NEGRO'S ORIGIN:

AND

IS THE NEGRO CURSED?

BY B. T TANNER.

PHILADELPHIA:

AFRICAN M. E. BOOK DEPOSITORY,

631 PINE STREET.

JAS. B. RODGERS CO.,
ELECTROTYPERS AND PRINTERS,
PHILADELPHIA.

THIS LITTLE PAMPHLET

IS

Dedicated

TO THE NEGRO,

WHOSE MANHOOD

CAN NEITHER BE DESTROYED

BY THE

RUST OF BARBARISM,

NOR THE

FIRES OF PERSECUTION.

LETTER FROM BISHOP CAMPBELL.

Rev. B. T. Tanner.

Dear Sir :—Allow me to say, that although I had not thought of writing an Introduction to your forthcoming Pamphlet, upon the "Negro's Origin," and "Is the Negro Cursed?" yet I had thought of writing an article which you might use with others of the same kind, and thus help forward the circulation of your little work. After seeing your notice in the Christian Recorder, I supposed that you were not waiting for me to accept the invitation you had given me to write the Introduction.

And now you must allow me to decline writing an Introduction. To write a proper Introduction to a work after the middle of the nineteenth century, a man ought to be well posted, not only as to the literary merits of the work itself, but also, as to the strength of the arguments produced against it by opposing theories.

As to the literary ability of your forthcoming Pamphlet, I am posted; but as to the strength of the arguments of many—very many opposing theories, I am not exactly posted. I must have time to compare your notes, with others who oppose, before I would be prepared to render a decision, which I would be willing to have go forth to the world in book form, to pass down to our posterity.

To say that I have read nothing, and thought nothing upon the subject, would be very far from the truth ; but

1* v

to say that I am prepared to defend all the arguments which you have produced, in opposition to the commonly received opinions, would be saying what is not the truth.

When you first named the subject of writing an Introduction, upon reflection of the subject, I thought it would be a good idea, for some one to write an Introduction for a second edition of the work, in which you would have a chance to enlarge, and the party introducing, would have a chance to examine, the sources of proof which you have introduced. By that means your work might not have only a transient existence, but it might possibly find a place among the few works that pass down from generation to generation. And such I desire to be the good fortune of your work.

Also, I hope in time to add something to the common stock, for which cause, I confess that I have to exercise a little caution about what I say and what I do.

I am yours truly,

J. P. CAMPBELL.

P. S. You must already be aware of the fact, that in my travels, I have no access to libraries, when away from my home; and that I am constantly preaching and doing Church business. Under such circumstances it would not be possible for an intelligent man, to write an intelligent Introduction to a Book. I am willing to help others, when I can really *help them, and help, or at least do no harm to myself at the same time.*

When I can write an Introduction for you, that will make the people call for a work from me, from what they see in that Introduction, I will then do it.

J. P. C.

1810 *Addison St., Phila., Pa.*

THE NEGRO'S ORIGIN.

L ET us search up the Negro's origin.
The inhabitants of the post-diluvian
world find their paternity in Noah, from
whose loins sprang Shem, and Ham, and
Japheth. Shem, in the Hebrew signifies "*renown, or a great name.*" Ham or Cham
signifies, "*warm or hot.*" Dr. Hale says,
"*black:*" Japheth or Yepheth, "*expanding,
widely spreading.*"

According to common chronology, Moses
wrote eight hundred and fifty-seven years
after the flood, and these are the names which
he gives to the patriarchs. The question is,
Did the fathers name their descendants? or
did the descendants name the fathers?

From the age in which Moses lived and wrote, as well as from the spirit of illumination which was in him, he knew the channels into which the three great tides of humanity flowed; and he doubtless named the sources of them accordingly.

The father of his own race, to whom the blessing of *renown* or *mastership* had been given, and which in a measure he already saw in the grandeur of the nations beyond the Euphrates, he called Shem: the father of the race upon whom the blessing of *enlargement* was to come, and which already began to have a fulfillment in the tribes of Japheth wandering to the expansive North-west, he called Japheth or Yepheth: the father of the black race that he saw inhabiting the hot Peninsula he named Ham or Cham. In keeping with our idea he named the father of that race whose prophetic servitude was about to commence, Canaan, for he shall bow the knee.*

Moses gazed upon the descendants of Ham and lo! they were all black, and he named their progenitor accordingly. To suppose that Ham was really black, is to suppose such a freak as nature has never received the

---

* Gesenius finds the root of this word in כָּנַע *to bend the knee.*

credit of performing. Albinos may indeed spring from blacks, but we have never read of blacks springing from other than negro stock. Ham was no more black, than Japheth was white; each doubtless was of a ruddy or clay color, which is undoubtedly the normal.* Both white and black are extreme colors.

Those Orientals alone, who live within a few degrees north of 40° N., and a few degrees south of 30° N—the locality doubtless of their creation, have maintained their normal color. Those tribes who strayed northward, brightened; those who strayed southward, blackened. This is the fact presented to our gaze to-day The reason whereof, whether of heat or cold, whether of condition or usage, we leave for others to decide.

What are the evidences that Ham and his descendants peopled Africa? We speak first of Ham.

I. Evidences, scriptural and historical, of Ham going into Africa.

(a) Scriptural evidence.

"And smote the first-born in Egypt, the

---

* The first man was called אָדָם i. e., Adam. This word denotes in Scripture "A man, a human being, male or female." The root of it is אָדַם, "to be red, ruddy," and was undoubtedly applied to man because of his ruddiness, or clay color, for in Hebrew all names are denotative.

chief of their strength in the land of Ham."
Ps. lxxviii. 51.

"Israel also came into Egypt, and Jacob
sojourned in the land of Ham." Ps. cv. 23.

"They forgat God their Saviour which had
done great things in Egypt; wondrous works
in the land of Ham, and terrible things by
the Red Sea." Ps. cvi. 21–22.

(b) Historical evidence.

We are told that Ham was a domestic name
for Egypt, and used by the Egyptians themselves anterior to the advent of the Hebrews.*

In Plutarch Egypt is called *Chemia.* An-
ciently there were cantons in Egypt denomi-
nated Psitta-*Chemmis,* Pso-*Chemmis.* In these
names the word Cham or Ham is easily dis-
cerned.

Herodotus, in Book **IV** Melpomene, speaks
of *Ammonians* or *Hammonians,* as keepers of
the temple of Theban Jupiter in Africa.
Rollin, deeply learned in North African
lore, says, "Ham was the second son of
Noah. When the family of the latter * * * *
dispersed themselves into different countries,
Ham retired to Africa; and it doubtless was
he, who afterwards was worshipped as a
god, under the name of Jupiter-*Ammon* or
Hammon." P iii. K. of E.

---

* See Gesenius חָם.

It is impossible to account for these marks, Scriptural and historical, on any other hypothesis, than the presence of Ham in Africa. No other continent claims him. No other continent presents the impress of his feet. The impress is genuine ; it is original ; let due credence be given.

II. Evidences, Scriptural and historical, of the sons of Ham going into Africa.

(A.) Cush is understood to have gone into Ethiopia. In Scripture wherever this word occurs, with the exception of Isaiah xi. 11, and Hab. iii. 7; and the places where it denotes a *person*, it is translated Ethiopia. If this be a proper translation, the settlement of Cush in Africa is assured, for the geographical position of Ethiopia is defined beyond controversy Is it a proper translation? That it is, appears from the following considerations.

(*a.*) The Cushim descended from Ham, and inhabited a hot south country Ham was in Africa, and his seed doubtless spread into the hot country of Ethiopia.

(*b.*) The Cushim were black. "Can the Ethiopian or Cushite change his skin?" Jer. xiii. 23.

(*c.*) The Cushim were in close proximity to the Egyptians, for the two are uniformly coupled together. See Isai. xx. 3, 4, 5; xliii. 3; Nah. iii. 9; Ps. lxviii. 31, etc.

(d.) Isai. (xviii. 2,) describes the Cushim as sending ambassadors in "vessels of bulrushes." Bulrushes * are purely an African or Nilotic production.

(e.) The country Cush was encompassed by the river Gihon. "And the name of the second river is Gihon, the same is it that compasseth the whole land of Ethiopia or Cush." Gen. ii. 13. Does not the Nile encompass Ethiopia? The decisive question is, Is the Nile that Gihon to which Moses referred?

In defending the proposition, The Nile is the Gihon; it should be borne in mind that such questions as the following are not to be heeded: If we thus affirm, will we not run counter to the opinions of a vast number of biblical critics? or, If we thus affirm, will we not spoil the refined conjectures of many over-curious divines? or, If we thus affirm, will it not be impossible to find even the vicinity of

---

* Herodotus says, in regard to the manner of building ships on the Nile, "They do not use timber artificially carved, but bind the planks together with the bark of the byblus (or bulrush) made into ropes."   *   *   *   *   *   *   *   *
" They have immense numbers of these vessels, and some of them of the burden of many thousand talents." *Euterpe,* xcvi.

the spot of man's first joys, and his first sorrows as well? He who searches for truth has little to do with consequences, which often stand like spectres to frighten men from their honest pursuits. Such souls have received the command, " Go forward," and nought remains but to obey. The single question here to be entertained is, Did Moses mean by the Gihon, his own familiar Nile? A common rule of criticism is, that an author must explain himself;* though it be to the confusion of all judges and commentators. Let Moses then interpret Moses. This is the more necessary, when we consider that after him, 500 years elapsed before another Scripture writer mentions the word, *Cush.* Job indeed mentions it, but his era is uncertain. The first after Moses was undoubtedly David.† If we credit the generations of these 500 years, with the same curiosity we ourselves possess, how were they to satisfy themselves with regard to the geographical position of the land encompassed by the Gihon? Must they not learn it from other

---

* Blackstone says, " In interpreting language in law, one method of interpretation is by comparison of one law with other laws which are made by the *same* legislator, and have some affinity to the subject."

† Ps. lxviii. 31.

2

portions of the Mosaic record? or else must
they not remain ignorant? Even so must we
learn from Moses the position of that Cush
which the Gihon encompassed. One may say
that the common knowledge of the earth, with
the positions of the several peoples as well,
would enable those generations to understand
the position of Cush. So let it be, and does not
that common knowledge as handed down by
tradition, point with a steady finger towards
African Ethiopia?

In what sense does Moses use the word
כּוּשׁ· i. e. *Cush* and its compounds? It appears
in his writings in the following places: Gen.
ii. 13; x. 6, 7, 8; Numb. xii. 1. In the
first of these, Gen. ii. 13, it is used as the
name of a country: "And the name of the
second river is Gihon, the same is it that compasseth the whole land of Ethiopia or Cush."
Where is that land? To which one of the
three great continents shall we look? Might
we not possibly find a ray of light in the name
it bears; knowing that in ancient times cities
and lands were invariably named after men?
After whom was the land of Cush or Ethiopia
named? Is there given us the name of such
an individual? and is it probable that he was
the first possessor of that land, and enjoyed

the prerogative of naming it? In Gen. x. 6, the very next place where the word is met, it denotes a person. "And the sons of Ham, Cush and Mizraim, Phut and Canaan." Cush a son of Ham. No other individual of the same name is mentioned in all the Scripture. Must we not conclude that if the land of Cush was named after an individual, as it most undoubtedly was, that individual was Cush, the son of Ham? Here then we have a first glimpse of the geographical position of that land. Ham was in Africa; the increase of his descendants made it necessary for them to spread abroad. Cush, the eldest, took up the march first, and penetrated the hot south country, and his grateful progeny called it Cush.

In Numb. xii. 1, where a compound of the word Cush is used, and which denotes a woman of the land, a Cushite, more and stronger light is afforded us to see the real position of the land. We read there, " And Miriam and Aaron spoke against Moses because of the Ethiopian woman (or Cushite) whom he had married, for he had married an Ethiopian woman." Did this Cushite woman belong to that land of Cush which Moses had previously mentioned, and which was encompassed by the Gihon? Did those German women, of whose virtue Tacitus wrote, belong to that Germany previously mentioned, and whose confines were encompassed by the Rhine?* Moses must interpret Moses, even as Tacitus must interpret Tacitus. The Cushite woman must be an inhabitant of the only land of Cush, which Moses mentioned, as the German women must be inhabitants of the only Germany Tacitus mentioned. Let us examine this matter more fully. The Cushite woman whom Moses married, whence came she? Moses must have married her, either in Egypt or in his tramp through Arabia. If he married her in Egypt, as tradition says, then may we know that her country was contiguous to Egypt, and may safely settle down on Ethiopia proper. If he married her while on the tramp through Arabia, from among the surrounding tribes, then must he have passed through her country This is the opinion of many The question then results in this,

---

* *Germania* xviii.

NOTE. We have a case exactly similar to this of Moses, in the history of Herodotus. In Book II. *Euterpe*, he speaks of the river *"Ister"* as commencing at the city of Pyrene, among the Celtæ, flows through the centre of Europe, and 'empties itself into the Euxine.' " Wherefore has the question long since been settled that this Ister is our modern Danube? Because the geographical and popular allusions of Herodotus demand it. Herodotus must define Herodotus. Even so Moses.

Ethiopia *versus* Arabia as the land of the Cushite. *But in all Arabia there is not a single river.*

To look for the land of Cush in far off Asia is most objectionable; if thus, how came this Cushite so far from home? How came she in the way of the great leader? And have not critics long since monopolized all the prominent rivers there found to make out the Pison, the Hiddekel, the Euphrates? The contest plainly lies between two. Let us settle it in haste. Cush is encompassed by the Gihon. Arabia is not encompassed by the Gihon, therefore Arabia is not Cush.*

That the Nile is the Gihon of Moses appears also from the name itself. Gihon in the Hebrew signifies† "A *stream, river,* so called as *breaking forth from fountains.*" It is from a verb which signifies to *break* or *burst forth.*

Does not Moses plainly allude to the annual *bursting forth* or *inundations* of the Nile, which

---

* Gesenius says, "Bochart with less caution than usual places the Cushites in a part of Arabia Felix; and with no better reason Michaelis makes them inhabitants, partly of Arabia, and partly of Ethiopia. But as Schulthers has justly remarked, there is no part of the Old Testament which makes it necessary to suppose that the Cushim were not in Africa. Indeed all the nations enumerated in Gen. x. 7, as sprung from Cush are to be sought in Africa.

† The word is גִּיחוֹן derived from the root גִּיחַ to *break* or *burst forth.*

have ever characterized it? Following the Hebrew idiom of naming things according to their quality, what other name would be so appropriate? It is thus the ancients have universally decided: Thus speaks the Septuagint;* thus speaks Josephus.† In the *Index Biblicus* of an authorized edition of the Vulgate we find this, "*Æthiopia, Africæ provincia, eam circumit fluvius Gehon.*" After a most thorough research Gesenius says, "By the river Gihon most probably the Ethiopian Nile is to be understood, which does in fact surround Ethiopia." The identity of the Nile with the Gihon conceded, as well also from the other proofs given, the advent of Cush into Africa is assured, and the translation of the word, *Ethiopia,* is fully justified.

B. In regard to the advent of the son Mizraim into Africa, the Scriptures speak most definitely   Indeed, Egypt is there only known by the name Mizraim. The word being dual it has been said of it, "Hence the dual Mizraim seems to have originally denoted upper and lower Egypt." Josephus says, "The memory also of the Mizraites is preserved in their name, for all who inhabit this

---

* Jer. ii. 18, Song of Sirach, xxiv. 27.

† Jos. B. I., 1, 3.

country (Judea) call Egypt, Mestre, and the Egyptians, Mestreans.[*]

Rollin says, "Mizraim settled in Egypt, which is generally called in Scripture after his name." And again, "Mizraim is allowed to be the same with Menes, whom all historians declare to be the first king of Egypt." The ancient name remains to this day among the Arabians, who call Egypt, Mesre. Although M. Basnage has ventured to express the opinion that Mizraim was never in Egypt, yet are his footprints too legible not to be deciphered.

(C.) As to the posterity of Phut settling in Africa, the evidence in Scripture is, that he is invariably joined with his brethren, the Cushites. Jeremiah xlvi. 9, says, " Cush and Phut that handle the shield." Ezekiel xxxviii. says, "Persia, Phut, and Cush with them." So also speaks the prophet Nahum. Josephus speaks as follows: " Phut also was the founder of Lybia, and called the inhabitants Phutites

---

[*] Jos. B. I., chap. vi. § 2.

NOTE. The Foulahs have a tradition that they are the descendants of Phut, the son of Ham.

Whether this tradition be true or not, it is a singular fact that they have prefixed this name to almost every district of any extent which they have ever occupied. They have Futa–Torro, near Senegal; Futa–Bondu and Futa–Jallon to the North-East of Sierra Leone.— *Wilson's Western Africa, page 79.*

from himself; there is also a river in the country of the Moors which bears that name, whence it is that we may see the greatest part of the Grecian historiographers mention that river and the adjoining country by the appellation of Phut."[*]

Pliny and Ptolemy mention places in North Africa called Phtemphu, Phtempti, Phtembute, which Calmet regards as originating in Phut. From such evidences, how could the world escape from the conclusion to which it has long since come, that Africa was peopled by Ham and his three sons, Cush, Mizraim, and Phut.

It is significant that not a trace of Canaan, neither in name nor ceremony, can be found on African soil. This is inexplicable, except upon the recognized hypothesis that he was never there. It is true that in the days of Athanasius, many of the peoples of North Africa claimed to have descended from the Canaanites, and their Punic tongue is said to have confirmed their assertion. But in that day Egypt had been greatly overrun by not a few of the Mediterranean nations. The native Hamites in that region, partook largely of the blood of the invaders. But these North Afri-

---

[*] Jos. B. I. vi. 2.

cans are not Africans proper, any more than
the whites in America are Americans proper.
The African of untainted blood, the Hamite,
pure and simple, is found to-day only in the
" woolly-headed negro," as Watson expresses
it, with a curl of the lip. Canaan in Africa is
an interloper. Since the day that he was
ostracised by his kindred for his irreverent
conduct to Noah, and forbidden to follow them
to their new home, lest they might partake of
his curse, Canaan has been to all truth an
Asiatic. There it was he lived, and there he
received upon his own pate, the full weight of
that curse, which felled him to the earth, and
ground him, as a distinct people, to dust. But
let him, if you will, be accounted among the
Africans of to-day, still is he not of the negroes, for all Africans are not negroes, though
all negroes are Africans.

To conclude; Africa is the land of Ham,
the Nile is the Gihon, Ethiopia the land of
Cush. To enter into particulars, as to the
precise period when the patriarchs migrated
thither, and the manner how, with subsequent
developments of government and society, would
be impossible, and conjectures are useless.
Living at this late day, only the mountain out-
lines of historical facts are seen. Let this suf-

fice. They are distinctly drawn; let us mount the high ridges and travel backward, but let us not presume to look down into the valleys, for dense fog will meet us. No people now exist who can trace more clearly their paternity than the negro. The genealogical table of the Jew, written upon the skin of beasts has perished, but the genealogical table of the negro, written in his own flesh, remains. Ages of scourging have not sufficed to erase it. Written by the finger of God, it is more enduring than the stones of Sinai. It remains, and will remain the badge of our suffering, the badge of our triumph.

Is the Negro Cursed?

THE answer to the question, Is the Negro cursed? depends altogether upon the answer given to the question, Is Ham cursed? If the Noachic cursings were really directed against Ham, then must his negro descendants prepare to take their full share. We acknowledge the validity of Noah's malediction. His reputed intemperance affects not its force. God's oracles are of his own choosing, and in no way can they affect the message which they may deliver. A tongue only is needed; whether it be in the head of a stupid ass, a lucre-loving Balaam or a drunken Noah, it is equally the Lord's mouth-piece. But the Scripture says of Noah: "And he awoke from his wine." Sleep invariably produces soberness, and the probability is that Noah was sober. The curses of Noah are valid—upon whom fell they, Ham or Canaan?

This question cannot be settled by consulting Jewish Talmuds, nor Targums, nor any of the sayings of the Rabbis. Nor can it be settled by consulting Christian doctors, ancient or modern, especially the latter, for in this case it has been seen, that even the most pious are susceptible of Race feeling, holding with kith and kin, be they right or wrong. Where may this matter be settled—where, definitely and impartially answer the interrogatory, Was Ham cursed? Only in the record written by Moses. If it cannot there be settled, it must forever remain unsettled, for all other records are to be laid aside.

The whole account, and the only account given is the following, found in Gen. ix. 18–27

18 ¶ And the sons of Noah that went forth from the ark, were Shem, and Ham, and Japheth: and Ham *is* the father of Canaan.

19 These *are* the three sons of Noah: and of them was the whole earth overspread.

20 And Noah began *to be* an husbandman, and he planted a vineyard;

21 And he drank of the wine, and was drunken, and he was uncovered within his tent.

22 And Ham the father of Canaan saw the nakedness of his father, and told his two brethren without.

23 And Shem and Japheth took a garment, and laid *it* upon both their shoulders, and went backward and covered the nakedness of their father : and their faces *were* backward, and they saw not their father's nakedness.

24 And Noah awoke from his wine, and knew what his younger son had done unto him.

25 And he said, Cursed *be* Canaan ; a servant of servants shall he be unto his brethren.

26 And he said, Blessed *be* the LORD GOD of Shem ; and Canaan shall be his servant.

27 God shall enlarge Japheth, and he shall dwell in the tents of Shem ; and Canaan shall be his servant.

Here we have the *Alpha* and *Omega* of this whole affair. He must grope in the dark, who is not satisfied with the light here offered. At the very commencement of our argument we say, and from our heart, would that all prejudice *pro* and *con* were laid aside, and that all minds were susceptible of arriving at the truth. Who was cursed, Ham or Canaan? We say CANAAN The proof we offer will be divided into Direct and Indirect.

Direct Proof.

(*a.*) The Scriptures say, CANAAN, in three distinct places. Ver. 25: " And he said Cursed be CANAAN." Verses 26 and 27 speak with the same precision—" And CANAAN shall be his servant."

By reason of this cursing Canaan must be

3

the guilty party, else the whole story goes for
nought. Having acknowledged the divinity
of Noah's malediction, it will not do to *suppose* Canaan to be *guilty ;* we must *know* it; at
least our faith in the justice of God will not
allow us to question his guilt for a moment.
God's cursings are always proof positive of
guilt. Our every conception of the Divine
character demands this. He cursed and destroyed all the ante-diluvian world. Do any
doubt their guilt? He cursed and destroyed
Sodom. Do any doubt its guilt? Are not all
His cursings, sufficient guarantees of guilt?
We know a portion of the angels sinned,
simply because they were not allowed to keep
their first estate. A Christian wants no better
proof. It is thus with Canaan. We know he
was the guilty party, because he was cursed;
and, we know he was the *only* guilty party,
because he was the only party cursed. That
he was cursed none pretend to deny; that he
was not the *only* person cursed, none can affirm. But if Ham was cursed by reason of
guilt, why should the whole burden of it
fall on Canaan? Why should Cush, and
Mizraim, and Phut go scot free? If some
transcriber has blundered and written Canaan
when he should have written Ham, then jus-

tice demands all his seed to take a share; and not the youngest and weakest bear the whole burden.

(*b.*) The Scriptures say again, " And Noah knew what his younger son had done unto him." That younger בן was Canaan, and not Ham, as we hope to be able to prove. Ham was not his younger son, as Scripture plainly informs us, in Gen. vi. 32; v. 10; x. 1; and 1 Chron. i. 4.

A fundamental rule of Scripture is to name children in the order of their birth. It would be useless to multiply instances. Nor is this rule ever departed from without an apparent reason. The sons of Noah are enumerated in the parts of Scripture just designated, and in each the well-known rule is observed, the familiar Shem, Ham and Japheth, is read.

Strong indeed must be the proof that demands us to break such conclusive testimony In regard to Ham there is not the least testimony offered, save that founded on the assumption that he is the party cursed; an argument *a posteriori* of the most shiftless kind. In regard to Shem and to Japheth, doubts may arise from the fact, that in the genealogical table of Noah's descendants recorded in 1 Chron. i. the children of Japheth are

given first, those of Shem, last; but Ham
keeps his middle place; also in Gen. x. 21 we
read, "And Shem * * * the brother of Japheth the elder." The word rendered "elder"
here, may indeed relate to seniority of birth;
but its primary and customary signification is
"*great*," of which multiplied instances could
be produced. Without extreme license the
declaration could be translated—"Japheth,
who is (to be) great." See Gesen. § 107
But why meddle with Japheth? Needs he a
defense, they are named legion who can give
it. Our business is with Ham; to see to it
that he be not displaced from his MIDDLE
position. Scripture awards it. Let no robber
hand efface it.*

We have thus seen from plain Scriptural
declaration that Ham was *not* the younger
בָ. We now proceed to show that Canaan *was*.

The Hebrew rendered by King James'
translators "his younger son," is בְּנוֹ הַקָּטָן.
With the translation given in the present

---

* Dr. Adam Clark says, " Ham was certainly the *youngest* of Noah,
and from what we read Chap. ix. 22, the *worst* of them; and how *he*
comes to be mentioned out of his natural order is not easy to be accounted for."

The Dr. here denies a plain statement of Scripture, and then ac-
knowledges that he cannot account for his own *supposition*. Like a
goodly part of the Dr's. comments, this was written under previously
conceived opinion.

text, an open conflict is the result. According to the ranking of the sons as given in Gen. v. 32; vi. 10; x. 1; 1 Chron. 1–4, Japheth is the youngest son; but that Japheth was not the transgressor is too apparent to need argument. How then can this plain contradiction be harmonized—how translate this Hebrew so as to meet the demands of truth, and yet harmonize the text? Can it be done? It most certainly can. The Hebrew words, denoting relationship, have a very wide latitude. The word אָב translated " father" in Gen. xix. 31, as well as in innumerable other places, is translated, " a grand-father," in Gen. xxviii. 13–31: and "great grand-father," in Num. xviii. 1–2. The word אֵם whose usual signification is " mother," is translated " grand-mother," 2 Kings xv 10. אָח " brother," signifies also, " a relative, kinsman, members of the same tribe, even a fellow-countryman." It is thus with the noun בֵּן " son." Standard authority says, " The word, *son*, like those of father and brother, is employed by the Hebrews in various other and wide senses." In Gen. xxix. 5, Laban is called the son of Nahor, when he really was grandson to the Patriarch. In Gen. xxxi. 28, grand-children are denoted by the same term, as also in verse

3*

55th of the same Chapter. In Ezra v. 1, the
prophet Zechariah is said to be the "son of
Iddo," when Zechariah himself declares he
was his "grand-son."

The same word has even a wider signification. The plural of it uniformly denotes "posterity, descendants." In the use of all these
nouns of relationship, the facts of the context
must define their limit; they themselves are
but general expressions of *some* kindred. Apply
this rule to Gen. ix. 24, and it will read—not
"his younger son," but "his younger grand-
son." This is perfectly allowable, as is shown,
while it gives harmony to the whole affair.
By reason of the punishment inflicted the crime
is fixed upon Canaan; and this fact of the
context fixes and defines the full scope of the
Hebrew, בֵּן. Canaan was the younger grand-
son as a matter of fact, and words must ever
accord with facts. But we would not have it
to be made read thus: let this take its part
with all other similar places found in our ven-
erable translation—let the context explain
here as elsewhere.

But, says one, the offense is plainly declared
to have been committed by Ham. We con-
tend that no offense can be proved from verse
22: "And Ham, the father of Canaan, saw the

nakedness of his father, and told his two brethren without."

Let us look at the incidents related. Noah had taken too freely of the juice of the grape, and in consequence was drunk. In this condition he made an immodest exhibition of himself. "*Et nudatus in tabernaculo suo.*" Now, what was the action of the children and grandchildren of their aged sire? criminal action? *Moses does not even intimate.* Ham, desiring to put an end to the reproachful exhibition, loses no time, but hastens to inform his brethren. But why did he not go himself demand his accusers? On the hypothesis that the party cursed, was the one of guilt, his course of proceeding was the most natural in the world. The conduct of Canaan is reported to him, he goes to see for himself, and his worst fears are more than realized. Having informed Shem and Japheth of the affair, he himself gives his attention to his irreverent son, while his brothers, assured of their father's nudity, go backward and cover him with a mantle.

If one will divest himself of prejudice, no blame can possibly be attached to Ham, by reason of what is declared in this verse. Must not the condition of the father come to the ears of the sons by some one? and must the bare fact of revealing the state of his father, incur guilt? If so, wo be to the angel messengers who carry back to Heaven the moral state of the world; for the world lies naked before God.

But Ham was not blessed as was Shem and Japheth, cries another accuser. Be it so. But he was not cursed ; neither was the blessing he received in common with his two brothers annulled. In gratitude to Shem and Japheth, their blessings are increased, but nothing is taken from Ham. Extra gifts do not detract from those given in common. Shem and Japheth were rewarded for a thoughtfulness and modesty, which Ham in the height of his indignation against Canaan neglected to make manifest. Very like indeed is his conduct to that of Moses at Meribah. Both manifested too much passion. But even in ascribing passion to Ham, it is to be taken for granted that he was satisfactorily made to know his father's condition, which can never be done. For ought to the contrary some of the children may have made complaint against Canaan, and like most parents it was not fully credited by his father till he saw for himself.

Indirect Evidence.

An indirect proof that Canaan is the guilty party is the notoriety he had among the people. This is evidenced in verse 18, *and before we are told a word in regard to the fall of Noah.* Verse 18, says, "And the sons of Noah that went forth of the ark, were Shem, Ham and Japheth; and Ham is the father of Canaan." All writings are for the purpose of giving information. To tell the Israelites who Shem was, Moses had no incident, or deed, known to the people, with which to connect his name. He must be known only as the son of Noah. It was likewise the same with Japheth. Neither directly nor indirectly were they connected with a popular notoriety. But it was not thus with Ham; aside from being the son of Noah, he was designated as the father of Canaan. A son of one noted individual, the father of another; but their notoriety was different. But who is Canaan? What had he done? Noah was known; he had done something, and in consequence had popular fame. Ham could be distinguished in no better way than to say that he was the son of Noah. But what was the force of the words—*the father of Canaan?* Shall the unknown identify the known? Is it reasonable to suppose, aye, is it possible that an obscure younger son could identify or designate a father; one of the four, too, saved in the Ark? It is impossible save on the hypothesis that he had done something, by which his name had become spread abroad. The following is not at all dissimilar in word and spirit: " And the sons of John (Adams) that went forth into the world were, John Quincy, Samuel, Josiah and Ebenezer, and John Quincy (Adams) is the brother of Ebenezer."

Likewise in verse 22, Ham is again designated as the father of Canaan. Canaan must have had a wide-spread notoriety; and the question presents itself, what had he done to achieve it? He was the youngest of four sons. The youngest do not usually have the greatest fame, all things being equal. Each of his three brothers were men of spirit; not likely to be overshadowed by a younger brother in deeds of moment. Each of them founded an empire; and living when the work of each is done, we are prepared to say that Canaan was the least likely to obtain an enviable fame of all the Hamitic family   Yet Ham is not designated as the father of Mizraim; though Mizraim was verily a prince; he is not designated as the father of Cush; though Cush reigned over Ethiopia, as Josephus says; he is not designated as the father of Phut. Would Moses give the Israelites and the world a clear designation of Ham, he points him out as the father of Canaan. Neither Scripture nor tradition give the least intimation of Canaan ever figuring in any capacity save that of a criminal, for which he was disgraced by his brethren, and cursed of God.

(*b.*) A second indirect proof that Canaan is the guilty party, is the significant fact that he did not accompany his father and brethren to Africa. That he did not is one of the best established facts of history and tradition: so patent indeed is it, that none pretend to advocate it. The most bitter slaveocrat has been compelled to acknowledge it. We go out of the regular train of argument to say here that the impossibility of locating Canaan in Africa, in no little measure accounts for the strenuous determination which the same slaveocrats have ever made to fix the crime on Ham; aye, it accounts for the ready acquiescence which many good men gave to the unjust imputation. Each of these classes looked upon the suffering negro; the conscience of the one upbraided him, and he would fain satisfy it by

making himself believe that God had doomed
his victim by an irrevocable curse; the
reason of the other, thought that surely where
such punishment was inflicted, there *must* be
some occasion.   Each saw that in some way
the father of the race was connected with a
divine curse, and though to him indefinite, it
yet gave satisfaction—satisfaction to the conscience of the one, satisfaction to the reason
of the other.   They saw not Canaan hitched
to this Juggernaut of torture and death; they
imagined they saw Ham.

The question is, Why did not Canaan and
his posterity accompany the tribes of Ham
into Africa? why this younger one remain?
In after years the twelve tribes of Jacob
marched up from Egypt—nor was one left
behind.   Why should not the four tribes of
Ham march down?   The youngest child is
most generally the pet, the best beloved.
Jacob loved Joseph better than all his brothers, because " he was the son of his old age."
Human nature is one.   Wherefore should
Ham leave this son of his old age behind?
The whole affair is inexplicable, without the
assumption that some sad transaction made it
necessary for them thus to act.   This we find
in the curse pronounced.   With this under-
standing how natural does their course become ?

how justifiable, in forsaking a brother, aye in *compelling* him to remain behind. These brethren had just experienced the wrath of the curse of God—had seen the floods descend, had heard the fountains of the deep break up, had felt the mighty throes of the earth beneath the feet of their angered God, and from the great depths of their souls they sighed to be spared from another such visitation. They could not doubt the prophetic dignity of their father. They knew his voice made known the will and mind of God, and when, in prophetic ecstacy they saw the roll of his eye and heard the muttering words, "Cursed be Canaan," they felt breaking asunder every tie of union and destiny. With one voice the brothers said, "Arise, let us go hence."

We conclude our argument by giving a *resume* of this sad drama. What is the part acted by each?—the definite part as given in the only credible account. What is it? without imagination, without supposition. The *personæ* of this drama, are, Noah, a father, and Shem, Ham and Japheth, sons; and Canaan, a grandson. What is the part acted by each? On the very face of the account it is apparent that all is not told. Our business in concluding this argument is not to meddle with

4

the untold, but to confine ourselves strictly to what is given us. Noah played the part of the drunkard. Ham makes known his condition to his brothers Shem and Japheth. Shem and Japheth, with the most commendable modesty, cover their father's shame, and Canaan is cursed. Thus briefly may the whole affair be told. The parts played by Noah, Shem, and Japheth, are doubtless given in full. A shade rests over the part enacted by Ham and his son Canaan. But as far as the action of these two are given, toward which does the account point as the guilty party? What is this account, howsoever indefinite? We have already been told Ham revealed his father's condition and Canaan was cursed. We admit the blackness of the shade as here met, yet peering into it as far as may be, like blind Samson, there is one pillar we may lay hold upon. The part took by Ham is uncertain, the part took by Canaan is uncertain, but the Spirit of inspiration, with whom there was no uncertainty, pronounced the curse on Canaan! and Ham went free. More conclusive evidence may be demanded by curiosity, but not by faith.

CANAAN cursed, the negro is free, the recipient of the common blessing pronounced—not by Noah under doubtful circumstances, but by God Himself.